Last Day, Hooray!

NANCY POYDAR

Holiday House / New York

Text and illustrations copyright © 2004 by Nancy Poydar
All Rights Reserved
Printed in the United States of America
The text typeface is Typography of Coop Light.
The art was created with gouache.
www.holidayhouse.com
First Edition

1 3 5 7 9 10 8 6 4 2

Library of Congress Cataloging-in-Publication Data
Poydar, Nancy
Last day, hooray! / by Nancy Poydar. – 1st ed.
p. cm.
Summary: On the last day of school, Ivy, her classmates, and teachers dream
of summer as they clean and prepare for the last party of the school year.
ISBN 0-8234-1807-3
[1. Schools – Fiction. 2. Parties – Fiction.] 1. Title.
PZ7.P8846Las 2004
[E] – dc21   2003047863

For Ms. Bell

It was almost summer, and all over town everyone was counting the days. "Four, three, two . . ."

"One day left!" squealed Ivy and Leah.

Miss Wheeler thought today would never come. Four, three, two, ONE!

At the brick building on the hill,
Mr. Masters checked his list.
One day left to get things done!

Mr. Handy whistled. One more day
to wipe footprints and spills!

Ms. Bell stuck flags in cupcakes.
Leah, Tyrone, Jody, Ryan . . . Ivy.
She knew their names by heart.

On the steps, Ivy pointed.

"Mr. Masters is the Lost and Found!"

"Eric's hat!" said Tyrone.

"Jolene's umbrella!" yelled Sophie.

"My knapsack!" Ivy giggled.

Henry had a surprise for Ms. Bell.

"I love surprises," said Leah.

"I hate good-byes," said Ivy.

Tyrone had a good-bye card from all of them.
"Sign this," he whispered to Leah.

"We can write to each other!" Ivy said.

Ms. Bell took down their pictures.
"We can talk on the phone!" said Leah.

"Cleaning time!" said Ms. Bell.
Leah pushed the broom.
Ivy held the dustpan.

Sharon sprayed
the cleaner.
Tom wiped the tables.

Mr. Masters collected the kickballs.

Ms. Bell stacked the books.

Mr. Handy emptied
the trash.

Ryan and Christy would take
home the fish.
"Good-bye, fishies," said Jolene.
She cleaned the tank with soap.

Warm bubbles drifted and floated like summer daydreams. Ivy's under-the-sprinkler daydream. Mr. Handy's at-the-ball-game daydream.

Ms. Bell's breakfast-in-bed daydream. Mr. Masters's vegetable-garden daydream.

Miss Wheeler's blue-bicycle daydream.

Leah's reading-with-her-Grandma daydream.
Ivy's playing-school daydream.

They cleaned
and dreamed
till recess, when
Tyrone yelled . . .

"Has everyone signed this card?"
Leah couldn't wait to hang the paper chains.
Ivy couldn't wait to give the cake to Ms. Bell.

After recess their room was bare. It smelled of cleaner.
No books on the shelves. No alphabet letters on the wall.
No kickball by the door.

Tyrone shouted, "Too quiet!"
Ivy sighed. "Too empty."
Leah whispered, "Time to decorate!"

Ivy loved making their room
beautiful once more.
   "Much better!" declared Leah.
   "Hide," hollered Tyrone.
"Here she comes!"

Ivy was writing on the board.
Dear Everybody, See you next fall!
Love, IVY
     Why?

Because it's the last day. Hooray! The school year is done.
Everyone's smarter. "Four . . . three . . . two . . . ONE!"